This book belongs to:

_____

Please be kind to this book!

FELIX
AND THE FLYING
SUITCASE ADVENTURE

Story by Annette Langen · Pictures by Constanza Droop

Translated by Marianne Martens

PARKLANE PUBLISHING

HAUPPAUGE, NEW YORK

Something very strange happened
when Sophie visited her Aunt Edda in
Germany. Her favorite stuffed bunny,
Felix, disappeared in the middle of the
night! This is how it happened.

Aunt Edda had taken Sophie and Felix
to an outdoor market. There were lots of
merchants there selling all sorts of interesting things. Sophie used her
allowance money to buy an old book of fairy tales. Aunt Edda spotted
a brightly colored handwoven rug.

"Ooooh, just what I've been
looking for," she said excitedly,
and Sophie helped her carry
the rug back home.

After dinner, Sophie read some of the fairy tales to Felix. Then they cuddled on the couch. Everything seemed perfectly normal.

But in the middle of the night Sophie was awakened by a loud bang.

The balcony door was open, and the curtains were blowing in the wind. Where was Felix? Why was the fairy tale book open on the floor? Sophie bent down to shut the book. Then she saw a picture of a man in a flying suitcase. Suddenly her heart started beating a little faster. There was no sign of Felix—or of his red plaid suitcase.

Sophie knew exactly what this meant. She and Felix had known each other forever—that is, ever since they'd been in the crib together. They were inseparable, except that Felix had a terrible travel bug. You never knew where he would end up next.

Felix had already sent Sophie letters from around the world. Once he had even landed on the moon. And he had traveled with a circus for a while.

"Oh, Felix," murmured Sophie softly, gazing into the night sky. "Why don't you ever take me with you?" She knew that her little bunny was off on a new adventure.

The next morning, Aunt Edda was shocked to hear what had happened in the middle of the night. "You just never know what to expect with that Felix of yours, do you?" she said. But before she could say anything else, the doorbell rang. It was the mailman, with an express letter for Sophie. Sophie couldn't believe it. The envelope said:

Eilzustellung
Exprès

Super Rush Express Mail
for my very best friend
in the whole wide world:
SOPHIE
c/o AUNT EDDA
CHAMISSOPLATZ 104
10965 BERLIN

Sophie was speechless. She gave the letter to Aunt Edda, who read it and said: "You know, Felix had a good idea. Why don't we go see the parliament building today?"

A little later, they were waiting in a long line to get in. Sophie felt like it took forever to get inside. But she was very excited to see the place where all the politicians meet, and the view from the glass dome was really

beautiful. Aunt Edda also showed Sophie where the Berlin Wall used to be. Germany was once a divided country. Sophie couldn't imagine that people from East Germany weren't allowed to travel into the West. "I'm so glad that something so bad doesn't exist anymore," she said, squeezing Aunt Edda's hand.

That evening, Sophie called her mother and father. When her mother asked her, "So what's new with you?" she had to fight back tears. "What's wrong, Sophie?" asked her mother. Sophie took a deep breath. "Felix has . . ." but she couldn't even continue.

Julius

Dad

Lena

Nicolas

Mom

Aunt Edda gently took the phone and told Sophie's mother all about the old fairy tale book, Felix's flying suitcase, and his letter. "Listen, Sophie, don't you worry," her father told her from the other end of the phone. "Your Felix will be back again before you know it. Just like he always is." Sophie nodded and wiped the tears away. But she really, really missed her bunny.

The days with Aunt Edda flew by. Soon it was time to take the plane back home. The whole family came to meet Sophie at the airport.

But what was that in her mother's hand? A letter! And the scratchy handwriting on the envelope said:

CREEPY MAIL FOR
SOPHIE
33 ELM ROAD
MANSFIELD, OHIO
U.S.A.

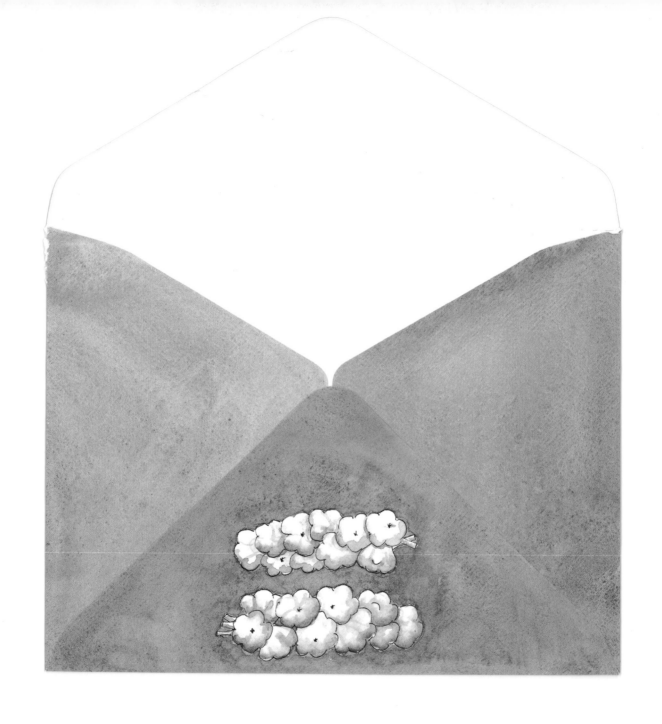

Yikes, thought Sophie, a real vampire castle! Now she wasn't feeling quite so upset that Felix had left her at home. Nicholas would really like this, she thought. Last Halloween he had dressed up as Dracula and he was obsessed with vampire stories. Sophie grabbed the letter and headed for her brother's room.

Sure enough, Nicholas was very excited. "I would have brought tons of garlic. It scares vampires, you know!" he said knowledgeably.

"I just hope the vampires know that," said Sophie. Then she headed for the stables to take her riding lesson.

Sophie's favorite pony,
Stella, sniffed curiously at her
jacket pocket. "Of course I've
brought you something," said Sophie,
offering Stella a piece of bread.

After her riding lesson, she went to the hayloft
to get a bale of hay for the ponies. The wind whistled
through the barn door, and spiderwebs stretched across
the rafters. It was a little creepy. Sophie tossed down the hay
bale and scooted down the ladder as fast as she could. But what
was that? Right in the barn door was a dark, winged figure. Sophie was
paralyzed with fear. "Woooooooooooohhh!" howled the figure and then,
switching to a friendly voice, asked, "So how was your riding lesson?"
It was only Nicholas in his vampire costume. Typical.

Every day after school, Sophie was in a huge rush to get home. "What is it with you?" puffed her best friend, Johanna. "Why do you have to run so fast?"

"I'm expecting mail from Felix!" called Sophie breathlessly. And sure enough, when she got home her mother handed her a new letter.

YET ANOTHER ☑
FOR MY LONG-LOST
SOPHIE
33 ELM ROAD
MANSFIELD, OHIO
U.S.A.

12.02.

YOUR VERY OWN FELIX :.
WHO L♥VES TO TRAVEL
CURRENTLY SOMEWHERE IN
➡ CALCUTTA, INDIA

What a different world, Sophie thought. She had already learned a little bit about India in school. Not too long ago her class had exchanged letters with a little girl from India named Kuni.

Sophie carefully pulled the picture Felix sent out of the envelope. He sure looked small in front of the Taj Mahal. Sophie looked at the picture for a long time and then she put it in a place of honor next to her bed so that he would be the first thing she saw every morning. What could Felix be up to now?

Lost in her thoughts, Sophie looked out the window. In the garden, she could see her cat, Kasimir, stalking through the bushes. She couldn't believe that her little Felix had been so close to a real tiger, the world's biggest predatory cat. When she thought about it, she really felt afraid.

That afternoon, when Sophie's friend Johanna came over, she told her all about Felix's trip to India. "I have a great idea," said Johanna. "Let's dress up in saris, like the Indian women wear." Up in the attic, they found a chest with an old curtain and some fabric in it. They ran into Sophie's room and hung the do-not-disturb sign on the door. They were very busy. It was a bit tricky to figure out the proper technique for wrapping saris. As a final touch, Johanna and Sophie made bracelets out of gold foil.

Mother was very impressed. "You two look like a couple of maharanis—that's what Indian princesses are called. But you're missing something." Taking red lipstick, she made a bindi dot right in the middle of their foreheads.

Many days passed before there was mail from Felix again. Sophie was really worried. What if Felix had lost his suitcase? Or what if he broke his paw and couldn't write to her? But at last a letter arrived.

Must go to the U.S.A.

28.02

LATEST NEWS JUST FOR

SOPHIE
33 ELM ROAD
MANSFIELD, OHIO
U.S.A.

Sophie giggled. She couldn't believe that Felix had almost had an accident with the Great Wall! When Grandma came to visit, Sophie slid down the banister and showed Grandma the letter.

"You know, your Felix is right," said Grandma. "The Great Wall has been there for over 2,000 years. It was originally built to protect China from its enemies. Even today, it's still the biggest single piece of construction ever created on earth."

"So China has a world record!" Sophie shouted. Grandma nodded and told Sophie that China has many world records. With more than a billion inhabitants, it is the most populated country on earth, and Chinese is the most widely spoken language in the world. Not only that, but China has Mount Everest, the tallest mountain in the world. Well, thought Sophie, I still hope my little Felix comes home soon!

The next afternoon, Sophie, her mother, and her grandmother sat on the floor and had some Chinese tea.

"I have a surprise for you," said Mom, handing Sophie a soft package. "I thought you'd like to have this since Felix is in China." Inside was a tiny panda doll.

"Oh thanks, Mom—he's so sweet!" She pressed her nose into its fur.

"Pandas live only in China," said Mom.

Sophie wanted to know all about pandas and went to look them up on the Internet. She learned that pandas were first discovered only 100 years ago in China's steep mountains. They're extremely shy and tend to hide in bamboo forests. At night, they eat lots of bamboo shoots. Sophie saw a picture of a panda mother with her baby and was very sad to read that pandas are an endangered species.

Sophie was just about to turn off her mother's computer when she noticed that a new email had just come in. She couldn't believe her eyes when she saw:

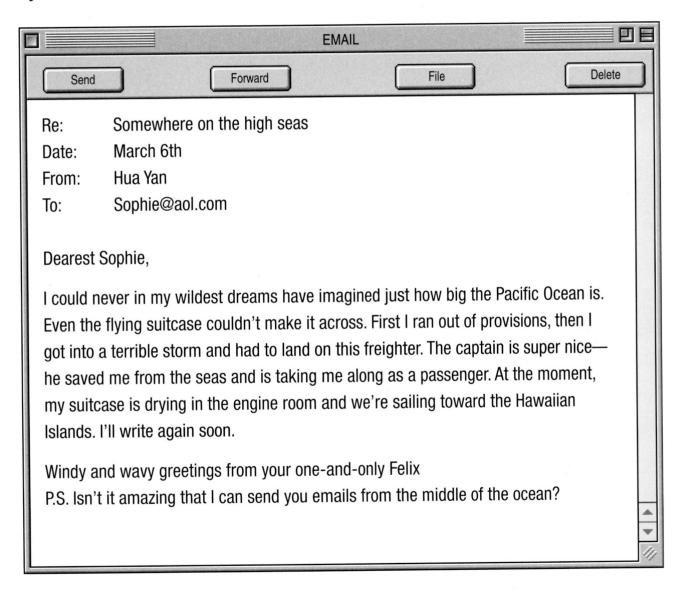

Re:	Somewhere on the high seas
Date:	March 6th
From:	Hua Yan
To:	Sophie@aol.com

Dearest Sophie,

I could never in my wildest dreams have imagined just how big the Pacific Ocean is. Even the flying suitcase couldn't make it across. First I ran out of provisions, then I got into a terrible storm and had to land on this freighter. The captain is super nice—he saved me from the seas and is taking me along as a passenger. At the moment, my suitcase is drying in the engine room and we're sailing toward the Hawaiian Islands. I'll write again soon.

Windy and wavy greetings from your one-and-only Felix
P.S. Isn't it amazing that I can send you emails from the middle of the ocean?

"Oh my goodness, that sure sounds scary," sighed Sophie. "He's lucky he didn't end up in a hurricane." Sophie grabbed her encyclopedia to look up hurricanes. She learned that hurricanes develop over warm oceans near the equator, then move around, become bigger, and can cause tremendous devastation when they hit shore.

Felix was lucky that the *Hua Yan* was close by, Sophie thought. She studied the globe that Felix had given her after one of his trips. She could see that the Pacific Ocean really was huge. The encyclopedia said that if you lumped together all the landmasses from the whole earth the total surface would still be much smaller than the Pacific Ocean.

"I would feel very lost at sea," thought Sophie, feeling very happy to have firm land under her feet.

世界遊　　　信封 5

Just before spring break when Sophie's family planned to go to the beach for vacation, another letter arrived from Felix. It seemed as though he'd already been traveling for ages, which wasn't surprising since the letter came from far away.

THIS IS A ☑ JUST FOR

S♥PHIE
33 ELM ROAD
MANSFIELD, OHIO
U.S.A.

Kukulkán Pyramid

"Dad!" shouted Sophie. "I always thought that pyramids were only in Egypt!" Dad told Sophie that different Indian tribes in Mexico and other South American countries built tremendous cities with huge temples and palaces that still hold many mysteries.

"Can you imagine," said Dad, "how the builders back then could calculate precisely how the setting sun would cast a shadow that looked like a snake sliding down the stairs." Sophie was amazed.

But the good news was that Felix was coming home soon! She was sure he was already on his way. Then she had an idea.

A little later Lena shouted, "Mom! Sophie took all the money out of her piggy bank!"

"Tattletale," mumbled Sophie, and then she walked down the street to the flower market. She bought some beautiful cactuses and was very careful not to prick herself with the needles. When she got back home, she made a tiny clay Felix and took him out to the sandbox. She put the cactuses down and built a little pyramid.

"Look, Lena! I've made the smallest Mexico in the world," Sophie said proudly. "If Felix has a little Mexico in his backyard he won't need to go there again!"

Several more weeks passed. Sophie often looked up in the sky, watching for Felix. But sadly, she didn't see the little rabbit in a flying suitcase. A week before Sophie's birthday, Dad brought a new letter from Felix. Sophie grabbed the letter and climbed up into her tree house to read it.

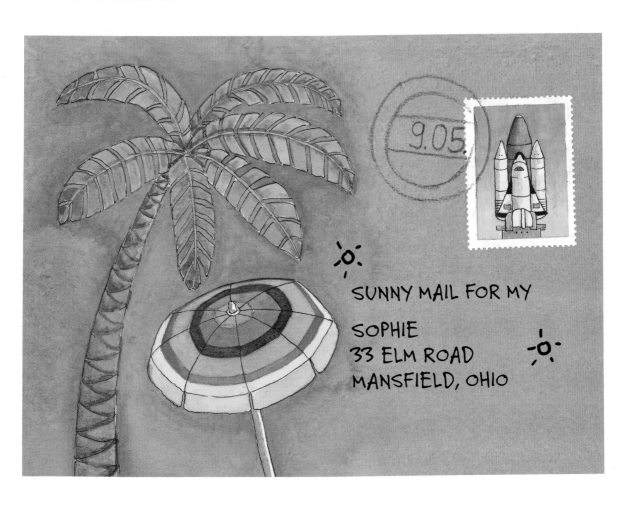

9.05

SUNNY MAIL FOR MY

SOPHIE
33 ELM ROAD
MANSFIELD, OHIO

FROM: FELIX
SOMEWHERE IN THE EVERGLADES
FLORIDA, USA

Florida Panther

Fox Squirrel

Raccoon

Purple Swamphen

Alligator

"Florida," murmured Sophie, picking up the envelope. A few grains of sand dropped out. She would have liked to join Felix at that sandy beach. But getting close to an alligator? No thanks, thought Sophie. If it really was nine feet long, it would reach up to her tree house.

"Sophie, where are you?" called Johanna, stomping around the garden in her new rubber boots. She climbed up the rope ladder. "So tell me," she said, "what do you want for your birthday?"

Sophie still had Felix's letter in her hand. "Take a guess!" she said.

Johanna laughed. "I know *exactly* what you want. It starts with an *f* and ends with *elix*!" And she was quite right.

Pelican

Swamp Turtle

Manatee

That weekend, Sophie's family went out to the country and rented canoes. They climbed in carefully and paddled off. On either side of the river were tall trees, thick bushes, and here and there you could glimpse a small boathouse.

Sophie imagined she was paddling through swamps in Florida with Felix.

"Watch out—there's an alligator!" she called. Lena gasped because there was a log in the water that looked just like an alligator!

On the morning of Sophie's birthday, there was still no sign of Felix.

Sophie was quite impatient in school, sliding back and forth in her chair. What if Felix arrived at home just now? She wouldn't be there to greet him.

Finally school was over. Mom made Sophie's favorite lunch, but Sophie was too excited to eat a bite. That afternoon, the doorbell kept ringing as Sophie's friends arrived for her birthday.

When all the guests arrived, Sophie's mom brought out the cake and everyone started to sing "Happy Birthday."

But wait! What was that strange sound outside?

Sophie ran out into the garden. There was Felix! He had landed his
flying suitcase on a little branch next to Sophie's tree house—but he
was about to fall!

"Don't worry, Felix!" Sophie yelled as she reached out her arms and
caught him. "Oh, Felix! I missed you so much!"

At the same moment, Sophie's grandmother grabbed a package that
fell out of Felix's suitcase. "I think Felix brought you a birthday present,"
said Grandmother.

Sophie unwrapped the package and inside was a pretty blue bandanna.

How strange, thought Sophie as she hugged her little bunny. Did Felix really fly all around the world? His suitcase looked just like any old suitcase—perhaps just a little dirtier. And Felix—he looked like a regular stuffed rabbit, too, didn't he?

But if he was just a regular stuffed rabbit, then how did he manage to bring Sophie the present?